To Aunt Cathy,
Love, Jack

Sept. 7, 1989

Sept. 7, 1989

To Aunt Cathy,
Love, Jack

How Many Days to America?

A THANKSGIVING STORY

by Eve Bunting
illustrated by Beth Peck

Clarion Books
TICKNOR & FIELDS: A HOUGHTON MIFFLIN COMPANY
New York

TO THE CHILDREN WHO CAME
and to Marilyn Carpenter who shared
their special stories.
—E.B.

For Mandy, David, Judy, and George
—B.P.

Clarion Books
Ticknor & Fields, a Houghton Mifflin Company
Text copyright © 1988 by Eve Bunting
Illustrations copyright © 1988 by Beth Peck
All rights reserved.
For information about permission to reproduce
selections from this book, write to Permissions,
Houghton Mifflin Company, 2 Park Street,
Boston, MA 02108
Printed in the U.S.A.

Library of Congress Cataloging-in-Publication Data
Bunting, Eve, 1928-
How many days to America? / Eve Bunting; illustrated by Beth
Peck.
p.   cm.
Summary: Refugees from a Caribbean island embark on a dangerous
boat trip to America where they have a special reason to celebrate
Thanksgiving.
ISBN 0-89919-521-0
[1. Refugees—Fiction.   2. Thanksgiving Day—Fiction.]   I. Peck,
Beth, ill.   II. Title.
PZ7.B91527Ho 1988
[E]—dc19
88-2590
AC

H   10   9   8   7   6   5   4   3   2   1

It was nice in our village. Till the night in October when the soldiers came.

My mother hid my little sister and me under the bed. When I peered out I could see my mother's feet in their black slippers and the great, muddy boots of the soldiers.

When they were gone my father said: "We must leave right now."

"Why?" I asked.

"Because we do not think the way they think, my son. Hurry!"

He would not let us take anything but a change of clothes.

My mother cried. "Leave all my things? My chair, where I sat to nurse our children? The bedcover that my mother made, every stitch by hand?"

"Nothing," my father said. "Just money to buy our way to America."

The word "America" was not new to me. I'd heard it whispered between my parents in the restless hours of the night. America. We were going there?

Others, too, moved silently along the secret streets.

Boats bobbed in the dark water off the quay and men talked behind their hands while gold passed from one pocket to another.

"I must have your wedding ring," my father told my mother. "And your garnets."

My mother took the ring from her finger and the garnet necklace from its little bag, buried deep in her bundle. She did not speak.

My father said we would leave while it was still dark.

"How many days to America?" my little sister asked.

"Not many," my father said. "Don't be afraid."

The fishing boat was small and there were many people. More kept coming, and more. We chugged heavily from harbor to open ocean.

"Can we see America yet, Papa?" All the *time* my little sister asks questions.

"Not yet," my father said.

We were an hour from shore when the motors stopped.
The men crowded the engines.

"A part is broken that cannot be fixed," my father told my mother, and her face twisted the way it did when she closed the door of our home for the last time.

The women made a sail by knotting clothes together and when they pulled it high I saw my father's Sunday shirt blowing in the wind. But the sail carried us back toward our own shore and men shot at us from the cliffs.

At last we got the boat turned in the right direction.

"How many days to America now?" my little sister asked.

"More, my small one," my father said and he held us close. I saw him look at my mother across our heads.

Day followed night and night, day. Our food and water ran out and many people were sick.

At sunset, my father and mother and sister and I huddled in the bow. Then my father sang as he sang at home.

"Sleep and dream, tomorrow comes
And we shall all be free."

That was the only time I was not afraid.

By day we fished and shared the catch. When it rained we caught the water in our buckets. I slept and dreamed. Of home. Of food. Of my favorite uncle who worked with my father in his shop and who had stayed behind. Sometimes I cried and then my mother would rock me against her.

Once we saw a whale, gray as an elephant and covered with barnacles.

"Come push us, whale," my mother called. "Push us to America."

But the whale did not hear.

Once a boat came, roaring close on wings of foam, and we were filled with joy. But not for long.

"Thieves!" Fear moved like a bad wind between us.

Men scrambled from the other boat to ours, waving their guns, shouting for money and jewels. There was little to take. But what we had went with them.

Once there was a shout of "Land!" and we crowded the railing. But though we pulled on the sail our boat would go no closer.

"We will swim for help," my father said and he and two others jumped into the water.

"No!" my mother cried.

But they were gone already.

When at last we saw them rise on the green roll of the surf, saw them carried to shore, we danced and cheered.

But there were soldiers on the rocks.

Everyone was quiet and my mother gripped my hand.

"They are bringing them back," she whispered.

Three soldiers with rifles came too, in the small boat. They brought us water and fruit, but they did not speak or smile as they tossed it up to our waiting hands.

"Was it not the right land, Papa?" I asked as the soldiers pulled away. "Will it not do?"

"It would do. But they will not take us," my father said.

My sister tugged at his arm. "They don't like us?"

"It is not that." He did not explain what it was.

Our family got two papayas and three lemons and a coconut with milk that tasted like flowers.

The sea was rough that night and my father's song lost itself in the wind. I said the words as the stars dipped and turned above our heads.

"Tomorrow comes, tomorrow comes,
And we shall all be free."

It was the next day, the tomorrow, that we sighted land again. I was afraid to hope.

A boat came. My mother clasped her hands and bent her head. Was she afraid to hope too?

The boat circled us twice and then a line was thrown and we were pulled toward shore.

There was such a silence among us then, such an anxious, watchful silence.

People waited on the dock.

"Welcome," they called. "Welcome to America."

That was when our silence turned to cheers.

"But how did they know we would come today?" my father asked.

"Perhaps people come every day," my mother said. "Perhaps they understand how it is for us."

There was a shed, warm from the sun on its tin roof. There were tables covered with food. Though the benches were crowded there was room for all of us.

"Do you know what day this is?" a woman asked me. She passed me a dinner plate.

"It is the coming-to-America day," I said.

She smiled. "Yes. And it is special for another reason, too. Today is Thanksgiving."

"What is that?" My little sister was shy, but not too shy to ask her questions.

"Long ago, unhappy people came here to start new lives," the woman said. "They celebrated by giving thanks."

My father nodded. "That is the only true way to celebrate."

We joined hands and closed our eyes while my father gave thanks that we were free, and safe and here.

"Can we stay, Papa?" my little sister asked.

"Yes, small one," my father said. "We can stay."